GRASSHOPPER
ON THE ROAD

by
ARNOLD LOBEL

An I CAN READ Book

HARPER & ROW, PUBLISHERS
New York, Hagerstown, San Francisco, London

For Kohar Alexanian

A portion of this book previously appeared in *Cricket*.

Library of Congress Cataloging in Publication Data
Lobel, Arnold.
    Grasshopper on the road.

    (An I can read book)
    SUMMARY: As Grasshopper sets out to follow a road,
he meets some unusual characters.
    [1. Animals—Fiction]   I. Title.
PZ7.L7795Gp 1978   [E]   77-25653
ISBN 0-06-023961-1
ISBN 0-06-023962-X lib. bdg.

GRASSHOPPER
ON THE ROAD

CONTENTS

Grasshopper wanted

to go on a journey.

"I will find a road," he said.

"I will follow that road

wherever it goes."

One morning Grasshopper

found a road.

It was long and dusty.

It went up hills

and down into valleys.

"This road looks fine to me,"

said Grasshopper.

"I am on my way!"

The Club

Grasshopper walked quickly

along the road.

He saw a sign

on the side of a tree.

The sign said

MORNING IS BEST.

Soon Grasshopper

saw another sign.

It said

THREE CHEERS FOR MORNING.

Grasshopper saw

a group of beetles.

They were singing and dancing.

They were carrying more signs.

"Good morning,"

said Grasshopper.

"Yes," said one

of the beetles.

"It is a good morning.

Every morning

is a good morning!"

The beetle carried a sign.

It said MAKE MINE MORNING.

"This is a meeting of the

We Love Morning Club,"

said the beetle.

"Every day we get together

to celebrate

another bright, fresh morning.

Grasshopper,

do you love morning?"

asked the beetle.

"Oh yes," said Grasshopper.

"Hooray!" shouted all the beetles.

"Grasshopper loves morning!"

"I knew it," said the beetle.

"I could tell by your kind face.

You are a morning lover."

The beetles made Grasshopper

a wreath of flowers.

They gave him a sign that said

MORNING IS TOPS.

"Now," they said,

"Grasshopper is in our club."

"When does the clover

sparkle with dew?" asked a beetle.

"In the morning!"

cried all the other beetles.

"When is the sunshine

yellow and new?"

asked the beetle.

"In the morning!"

cried all the other beetles.

They turned somersaults

and stood on their heads.

They danced and sang.

"M–O–R–N–I–N–G

spells morning!"

13

"I love afternoon too,"

said Grasshopper.

The beetles stopped

singing and dancing.

"What did you say?" they asked.

"I said that I loved afternoon,"

said Grasshopper.

All the beetles were quiet.

"And night is very nice,"

said Grasshopper.

"Stupid," said a beetle.

He grabbed the wreath of flowers.

"Dummy," said another beetle.

He snatched the sign

from Grasshopper.

"Anyone who loves

afternoon and night

can never, never

be in our club!"

said a third beetle.

"UP WITH MORNING!"

shouted all the beetles.

They waved their signs

and marched away.

Grasshopper was alone.

He saw the yellow sunshine.

He saw the dew

sparkling on the clover.

And he went on down the road.

A New House

The road went up a steep hill.

Grasshopper climbed to the top.

He found a large apple

lying on the ground.

"I will have my lunch,"

said Grasshopper.

He ate a big bite of the apple.

"Look what you did!" said a worm,

who lived in the apple.

"You have made a hole in my roof!"

"It is not polite

to eat a person's house,"

said the worm.

"I am sorry," said Grasshopper.

Just then the apple

began to roll down the road

on the other side of the hill.

"Stop me! Catch me!"

cried the worm.

The apple was rolling

faster and faster.

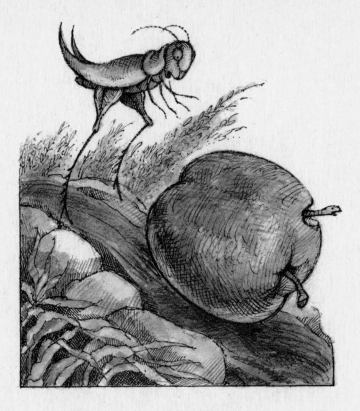

"Help, my head

is bumping on the walls!

My dishes are falling

off the shelf!"

cried the worm.

19

Grasshopper ran

after the apple.

"Everything is a mess in here!"

cried the worm.

"My bathtub is

in the living room.

My bed is in the kitchen!"

Grasshopper

kept running

down the hill.

But he could not catch

the apple.

"I am getting dizzy,"

cried the worm.

"My floor is on the ceiling!

My attic is in the cellar!"

The apple

rolled and rolled.

It rolled all the way down

to the bottom of the hill.

The apple hit a tree.

It smashed

into a hundred pieces.

"Too bad, worm,"

said Grasshopper.

"Your house is gone."

The worm

climbed up

the side

of the tree.

"Oh, never mind,"

said the worm.

"It was old,

and it had a big bite

in it anyway.

This is a fine time

for me to find a new house."

Grasshopper looked up
into the tree.
He saw that it was filled
with apples.
Grasshopper smiled,
and he went on down the road.

The Sweeper

Grasshopper saw

a cloud of dust.

"Clean, clean, clean,"

said a housefly,

who was sweeping the road.

"My broom and I

will make this road

as clean as can be."

"Housefly," said Grasshopper,

"the road is not very dirty."

"It is much too dusty,"

said the housefly.

"It is covered

with stones and sticks

and other nasty things.

My broom and I

will brush them all away."

The housefly went on sweeping.

"One day I was at home,

not doing much of anything,"

said the housefly.

"I saw a speck of dust on my rug.

I picked up the speck of dust.

Next to it was

another speck of dust.

I picked up that one, too."

"Next to that speck of dust

was another speck of dust.

I ran and got my broom.

I swept up

all the dust

that was on my rug.

Then I saw a piece of dirt

on my floor.

Next to it

was another piece of dirt.

And next to that

was another piece of dirt.

With my broom

I swept up all the dirt

that was on my floor."

"I cleaned my whole house

from top to bottom.

I even washed my windows.

After I washed them,

I looked outside.

I saw my garden path.

There were ugly pebbles

on my garden path.

I rushed outside with my broom.

I swept all the pebbles away.

At the end of the path

was my gate.

It was covered

with mud and moss.

I scrubbed

all the mud and moss

off my gate.

I opened the gate

and walked out onto

this dusty, dirty road."

"I took my broom

and went sweep, sweep, sweep

up the road," said the housefly.

"You have worked very hard,"

said Grasshopper.

"I think that you

should rest for a while."

"No, no, no," said the housefly.

"I will never rest.

I am having a wonderful time.

I will sweep

until the whole world

is clean, clean, clean!"

The dust was getting

into Grasshopper's eyes.

So he said good-bye

to the housefly,

and he went on

down the road.

The Voyage

Grasshopper came

to a puddle of water

in the road.

He was just about

to hop over the puddle.

"Wait!" cried a tiny voice.

Grasshopper looked down.

At the edge of the puddle

was a mosquito.

He was sitting in a little boat.

"It is a rule," said the mosquito.

"You must use

this ferry boat

to get across the lake."

"But sir,"

said Grasshopper,

"I can easily jump over

to the other side."

"Rules are rules,"

said the mosquito.

"Climb into my boat."

"Your boat is too small for me,"

said Grasshopper.

"Rules are rules,"

said the mosquito.

"You *must*

get into my boat!"

"I can't fit

into your boat,"

said Grasshopper.

"Rules are still rules!"

shouted the mosquito.

"Well then," said Grasshopper,

"there is only one thing

for me to do."

Grasshopper picked up the boat.

"All aboard,"

called the mosquito.

Grasshopper held the boat

very carefully.

He stepped into the puddle.

"You are lucky

to be with me

on this voyage,"

said the mosquito.

"I have been sailing

back and forth

across this lake

for many years,"

said the mosquito.

"I am not afraid

of storms or waves."

Grasshopper took another step.

"I know more

about sailing

than anyone else around here,"

said the mosquito.

Grasshopper took

one more step.

He was on

the other side

of the puddle.

He put the boat

down into the water.

"That was a good trip,"

said the mosquito.

"Now I must hurry back

to the other shore

to wait for new riders."

41

"Thank you," said Grasshopper.

"Thank you very much
for taking me
safely across the lake."

"I was glad to do it,"
said the mosquito.

Grasshopper waved good-bye
and kept on
walking down the road.

Always

In the late afternoon

Grasshopper saw a mushroom.

It was growing

at the edge of the road.

"I will rest my feet," he said.

Grasshopper sat on the mushroom.

Three butterflies flew down.

"Grasshopper,"

said the butterflies,

"you will have to move."

"Yes," said the first butterfly.

"You are sitting on our place.

Every afternoon at this time,

we fly to this mushroom.

We sit down on it for a while."

"There are lots of other mushrooms,"

said Grasshopper.

"They will not do,"

said the second butterfly.

"This is the mushroom

we *always* sit on."

Grasshopper got up.

The three butterflies sat down.

"Each and every day
we do the same thing
at the same time,"
said the third butterfly.
"We like it that way."
"We wake up in the morning,"
said the first butterfly.
"We scratch our heads three times."

"Always," said the second butterfly.

"Then we open and close our wings

four times.

We fly in a circle six times."

"Always," said the third butterfly.

"We go to the same tree

and eat the same lunch every day."

"Always," said the first butterfly.

"After lunch we sit

on the same sunflower.

We take the same nap.

We have the same dream.

"What sort of dream?"

asked Grasshopper.

"We dream that

we are sitting

on a sunflower

taking a nap,"

said the second

butterfly.

"Always," said the third butterfly.

"When we wake up,

we scratch our heads

three more times.

We fly in a circle six more times."

"Then we come here,"

said the first butterfly.

"We sit down on *this* mushroom."

"Always," said the second butterfly.

"Don't you ever change anything?"

asked Grasshopper.

"No, never," said the butterflies.

"Each day is fine for us."

50

"Grasshopper,"

said the butterflies,

"we like talking to you.

We will meet you

every day at this time.

We will sit on this mushroom.

You will sit right there.

We will tell you all about

our scratching and our flying.

We will tell you all about

our napping and our dreaming.

You will listen just the way

you are listening now."

"No," said Grasshopper.

"I am sorry,

but I will not be here.

I will be moving on.

I will be doing new things."

"That is too bad,"

said the butterflies.

"We will miss you.

Grasshopper, do you really

do something *different*

every day of your life?"

"Always," said Grasshopper.

"Always and always!"

He said good-bye
to the butterflies
and walked quickly
down the road.

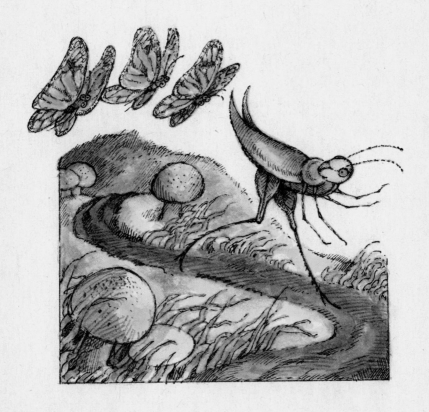

At Evening

In the evening

Grasshopper walked slowly

along the road.

The sun was going down.

The world was soft and quiet.

Grasshopper heard

a loud sound.

ZOOM!

Grasshopper heard

another noise.

ZOOOM!

He saw two dragonflies

in the air.

"Poor Grasshopper,"

said the dragonflies.

"We are flying fast.

You are only walking.

That is very sad."

"It is not sad,"

said Grasshopper.

"I like to walk."

The dragonflies flew

over Grasshopper's head.

"We can see so many things

from up here,"

said the dragonflies.

"All you can see

is that road."

"I like this road,"

said Grasshopper.

"And I can see

flowers growing

along the side of the road."

56

"We are zipping
and zooming,"
said the first dragonfly.
"We do not have time
to look at flowers."

"I can see leaves

moving in the trees,"

said Grasshopper.

"We are looping

and spinning,"

said the second dragonfly.

"We do not have time

to look at leaves."

58

"I can see the sunset

over the mountains,"

said Grasshopper.

"What sunset?

What mountains?"

asked the dragonflies.

"We are diving and dipping.

There is no time

to look at sunsets and mountains."

ZOOOOM!

The two dragonflies

raced across the sky.

Soon they were gone.

The world was quiet again.

The sky became dark.

Grasshopper watched the moon

rising over the land.

He watched the stars come out.

He was happy

to be walking slowly

down the road.

Grasshopper was tired.

He lay down in a soft place.

He knew that in the morning

the road would still be there,

taking him on and on

to wherever

he wanted to go.